JANET MCNAUGHTON ◆ ART BY SUSAN TOOKE

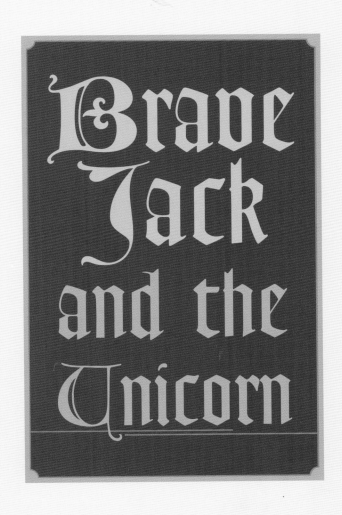

TUNDRA BOOKS

Published in Canada by Tundra Books,
75 Sherbourne Street, Toronto, Ontario M5A 2P9

Published in the United States by Tundra Books of Northern New York,
P.O. Box 1030, Plattsburgh, New York 12901

Library of Congress Control Number: 2004110123

Library and Archives Canada Cataloguing in Publication

McNaughton, Janet, 1953-

    Brave Jack and the unicorn / Janet McNaughton; Susan Tooke, illustrator.

ISBN 0-88776-677-3

    I. Tooke, Susan II. Title.

PS8575.N385B73 2005   jC813'.54   C2004-904117-7

We acknowledge the financial support of the Government of Canada through the Book Publishing
Industry Development Program (BPIDP) and that of the Government of Ontario through the
Ontario Media Development Corporation's Ontario Book Initiative. We further acknowledge the
support of the Canada Council for the Arts and the Ontario Arts Council for our publishing program.

ONTARIO ARTS COUNCIL
CONSEIL DES ARTS DE L'ONTARIO

The illustrator acknowledges the support of the Province of Nova Scotia through the Department of Tourism,
Culture and Heritage.

Medium: Acrylic on watercolor paper

Printed in Hong Kong, China

2 3 4 5 6 7   10 09 08 07 06 05

Locations of Illustrations, Newfoundland, Canada

1. Pouch Cove, Avalon Peninsula
2. New Melbourne, Trinity Bay
3. New Chelsea, Trinity Bay
4. Grates Cove, Trinity Bay
5. New Melbourne, Trinity Bay
6. Salvage, Bonavista Bay
7. Near Daniel's Cove, Trinity Bay
8. Cabot Tower, Signal Hill, the Anglican Cathedral of St. John the Baptist, St. John's
9. The Crypt, the Anglican Cathedral of St. John the Baptist, St. John's
10. Cape St. George, Port au Port Peninsula
11. Near Bakers Brook, Bonne Bay
12. Green Point, Gros Morne National Park
13. The Tablelands, Gros Morne National Park
14. The Arches, Northern Peninsula
15. Torbay Newfoundland Pony Project, Avalon Peninsula

For my daughter, Elizabeth, and all the children of Newfoundland

and Labrador, at home and away

J.M.

For my princess, my daughter Beth Crichton, with love

S.T.

ACKNOWLEDGMENTS

This story was inspired by listening to actor Andy Jones tell Newfoundland
folktales while I was working with him and students of Macdonald Drive Junior High
on an Arts Smarts project in 2000. Andy's tales were previously collected from
Pius Power Senior of Clattis Harbour, Placentia Bay, and adapted from
Folktales of Newfoundland, edited by Herbert Halpert and John Widdowson.
I also drew on *Little Jack and Other Newfoundland Folktales,* edited by John Widdowson,
and *Complete Fairy Tales of the Brothers Grimm,* edited by Jack Zipes.
The chase sequence was adapted from a story I heard from the late Émile Benoît,
Newfoundland fiddler and raconteur extraordinaire.

JANET McNAUGHTON

I would like to thank The Society for Creative Anachronism, Barony of Ruantallan;
The Ross Farm Museum; Deannie Sullivan Fraser; Janet McNaughton;
Ben Dalton (Jack); and Star, the Newfoundland pony, for their gracious support.

SUSAN TOOKE

In a little cove by the sea lived an old widow with three sons. Tom, the eldest, was as handsome as the day. The middle son, Bill, was as clever as a cat. But the youngest, Jack, was neither handsome nor clever, and gave his mother much trouble besides. When she sent him to town to sell the turnips, he gave away half to beggars.

"Why would you do such a thing?" his mother cried.

"I couldn't bear to see them hungry," Jack replied.

His brothers laughed. "Tom's face may win his fortune," his mother said, "and Bill has his wits. But you, Jack, will never amount to anything."

"That's the truth of it," said Jack, with a smile.

"Too kindhearted to pull weeds from the potatoes," Jack's brothers teased, and they treated him like a servant, giving him the jobs no one wanted. Jack cleaned the chicken coop and slept in the barn when a cow was sick. But he always had a kind word for everyone.

"Jack is nothing but a fool," his brothers told anyone who would listen.

One day, Tom said, "Why should I break my back on this farm? Mother, buy me a suit of clothes. I'm off to seek my fortune."

The old widow spent her life's savings on clothing and a fine bay stallion for Tom. When he left, she wept bitterly. "Good-bye, my handsome son," she cried. "May angels guide your way." And off rode her eldest without a backward glance.

When Tom left, Bill began to frown. Soon he said, "Mother, I've a mind to seek my fortune too. You owe me as much as you gave Tom."

The old widow agreed. "I'll sell half my land and livestock so you can go into the world like a gentleman." And so she bought Bill clothes that were just as fine as Tom's and a milk white mare to carry him. She wept bitterly when Bill left. "Good-bye, my clever son," she said. "May kindly spirits guide your path." And off rode Bill without a backward glance.

Jack was too kindhearted to kill the animals, so that winter he and his mother made do with the food he grew and salt fish the fishermen gave him.

Next spring, when the ice was out of the harbor, Jack's mother said, "We haven't heard from your brothers. Perhaps they've come to harm. Jack, go find them, if you can."

"Bake me a loaf of bread then, Mother, and give me some cheese, and I'll be on my way." And off Jack went in his old clothes with a hole in his boot, carrying a little satchel. His mother shed no tears to see him go.

Near sunset, Jack came to a rushing stream. *I'll pass the night here,* he thought. As he broke his bread, he noticed some ants. Thinking they must be hungry too, Jack gave them a crumb of bread. It pleased him to see the ants enjoy their feast.

That night, the queen of the ants came to Jack in a dream. "You have been kind to us," she said, "where others were cruel. If you need help, just blow this whistle and we'll come."

What a strange dream, Jack thought when he woke, but in his hand was a silver whistle. "Who would need help from the ants?" he said, but he put the whistle away safely all the same.

That morning, Jack came to a great apple tree, covered in ripe red apples even though it was spring. *What luck,* Jack thought. Then he noticed an axe, lodged deep in the trunk. "That must hurt the tree," Jack said aloud, and he freed the axe, though it took him all morning. When Jack finally reached for an apple, it was heavy as stone. "This apple seems to be made of gold!" Jack cried. He looked up. All the apples were gold. Jack turned back to the road, putting the gold apple in his pocket for it didn't seem right to leave it behind. "More's the pity," Jack sighed, "for I longed to taste an apple."

Just then something fell behind him. When Jack looked back, one perfect red apple lay under the tree. "Now, that's more to my liking," he said. After Jack ate the sweet and juicy apple, he found he wasn't hungry. He walked the rest of the day and slept the night without eating.

In the morning Jack still wasn't hungry, so he walked on without breakfast. Around midday, he spied a woman by the road, bent double over her sewing.

"Young man," she said, "could you spare some food? For I have sewn for seven weeks and seven days."

"I'm happy to share," Jack said. They ate all the bread and half the cheese. "Take this cheese, for it would break my heart to leave you without food," Jack said when it was time to go.

The woman smiled. "I believe you're the one I've been waiting for. Try this on." The coat she gave him was the best Jack had ever seen, far better than his brothers' finery. It fit perfectly besides.

This coat is too good for a simple lad like me, Jack thought. *Besides, the woman would eat well with the money its sale would fetch.* But, when Jack looked, she was gone. "Perhaps I'll find her up ahead," he said.

Jack stuffed his old clothes into his satchel, putting the silver whistle and the apple of gold into the pocket of his new coat. He felt strange in his finery, but stranger still when he looked down at the hole in his boot.

Where the woods gave way to meadows of hay, Jack heard a terrible cry. *That's the bawling of a sick cow,* Jack thought, walking to a little barn to investigate.

When the farmer saw Jack in his fine coat, he said, "Forgive me, young gentleman, if my cow disturbed you, for she has labored to give birth a night and a day."

"Perhaps I can help," said Jack. Slipping off his new coat, he set to work, turning the calf right way around. In no time, a fine baby calf stood on wobbly legs beside her mother.

"I fear you've ruined your boots helping me," the farmer said when they were finished.

Jack smiled. "I've been ruining these boots for years."

"Still," the farmer said, "you saved my livelihood. Stay the night and share my supper."

"That I will," Jack said, happy for the company.

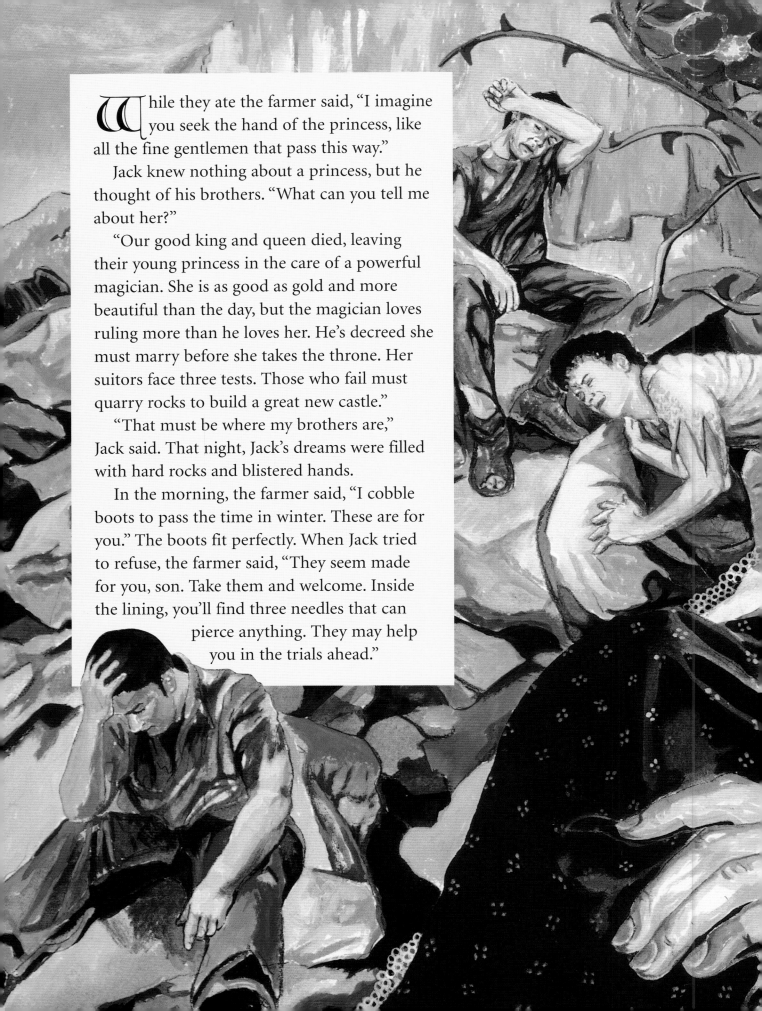

While they ate the farmer said, "I imagine you seek the hand of the princess, like all the fine gentlemen that pass this way."

Jack knew nothing about a princess, but he thought of his brothers. "What can you tell me about her?"

"Our good king and queen died, leaving their young princess in the care of a powerful magician. She is as good as gold and more beautiful than the day, but the magician loves ruling more than he loves her. He's decreed she must marry before she takes the throne. Her suitors face three tests. Those who fail must quarry rocks to build a great new castle."

"That must be where my brothers are," Jack said. That night, Jack's dreams were filled with hard rocks and blistered hands.

In the morning, the farmer said, "I cobble boots to pass the time in winter. These are for you." The boots fit perfectly. When Jack tried to refuse, the farmer said, "They seem made for you, son. Take them and welcome. Inside the lining, you'll find three needles that can pierce anything. They may help you in the trials ahead."

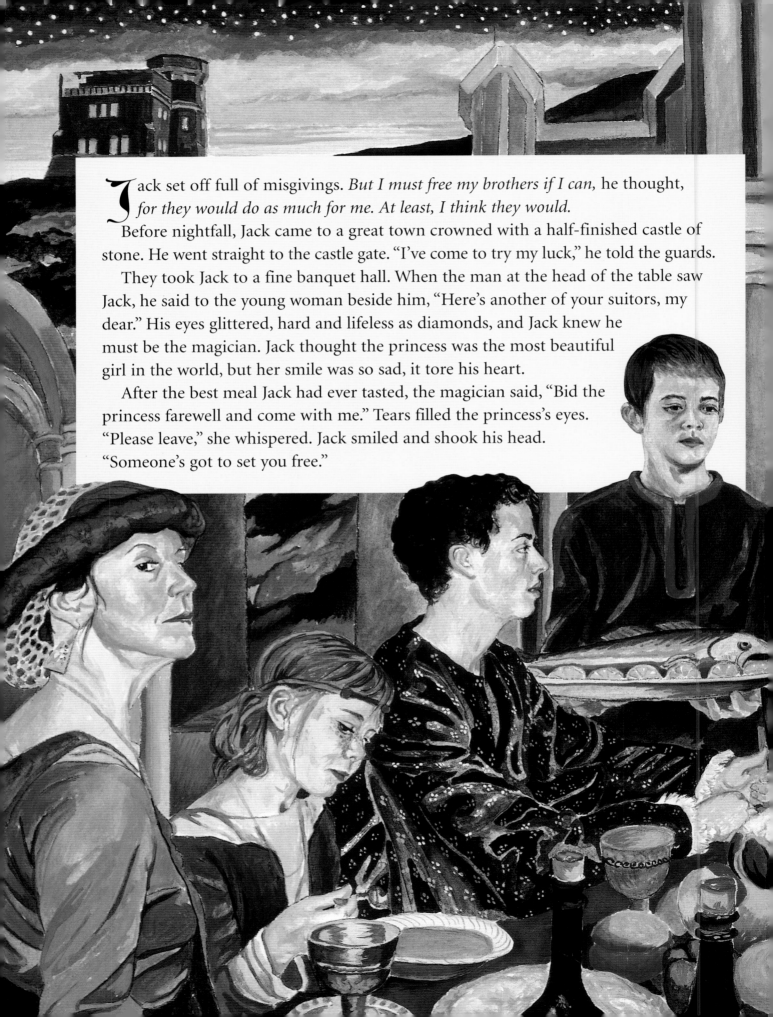

$\mathcal{J}$ack set off full of misgivings. *But I must free my brothers if I can,* he thought, *for they would do as much for me. At least, I think they would.*

Before nightfall, Jack came to a great town crowned with a half-finished castle of stone. He went straight to the castle gate. "I've come to try my luck," he told the guards.

They took Jack to a fine banquet hall. When the man at the head of the table saw Jack, he said to the young woman beside him, "Here's another of your suitors, my dear." His eyes glittered, hard and lifeless as diamonds, and Jack knew he must be the magician. Jack thought the princess was the most beautiful girl in the world, but her smile was so sad, it tore his heart.

After the best meal Jack had ever tasted, the magician said, "Bid the princess farewell and come with me." Tears filled the princess's eyes. "Please leave," she whispered. Jack smiled and shook his head. "Someone's got to set you free."

The magician led Jack down into the chilly foundations of the castle. A massive door swung open. In the torchlight, Jack saw the room was filled with wheat. "Not wheat alone," the magician said, as if he'd read Jack's mind. "This wheat is filled with sand. Separate the wheat from the sand before sunrise. If you fail, you're off to the quarry."

When the door closed, Jack sank to the floor. *How foolish was I to think I could win the day where others failed.* After a while, he remembered the whistle in his pocket. *Perhaps a tune would cheer me,* he thought. The whistle made poor music indeed, but before Jack stopped, thousands of ants streamed into the room.

Jack recognized the queen of the ants from his dream. "How can we help?" she said. Jack explained his plight. "Never fear," said the queen, and she ordered her little subjects to work.

In the morning, the magician found a huge hill of wheat on one side of the room and a huge hill of sand on the other. He only frowned and said, "Now you must pass the second test."

ithout so much as breakfast, the magician took Jack to the edge of the sea. Through the fog, a great mountain glittered in the sun. "It looks like glass," Jack said.

"It is," replied the magician. "A flower grows at the top. Bring it back before sunset, or you're off to the quarry." And he left Jack alone.

"My fine new boots won't help me now," Jack said, but then he remembered the needles. His heart sank when he saw them, for they looked like any other needles. But they pierced the glass as if it were butter. With the help of the needles, Jack pulled himself up the mountain. More than once he thought he would fall to his death, but soon he was back in the castle with the flower in hand.

The magician was not pleased. "That was only the second test," he said. "Now, you must pass the third."

"Wait," the princess cried, "Jack must have food and rest first, for he has worked a night and a day." It cheered Jack to find the princess so kindhearted.

After a good meal and a nap, Jack was taken to the edge of a vast forest at sunset.

"In these woods lives a unicorn," the magician said. "Find him before sunrise. I don't doubt you'll be in the quarry tomorrow, unless you lose your way in the woods forever." With a harsh laugh, he was gone.

Jack's courage failed, but after a time, the moon rose and he took heart. "At least I can see my way," he said.

Just then, someone called, "Jack, come here quickly!" It was the princess. "The magician can never find the unicorn himself. Only a kind heart can. But if you give the unicorn to him, he will rule forever." She sighed. "In any case, to tame the unicorn, you need a gold apple from the Tree of Compassion. I fear you are bound for the quarry like all the others. And I like you best."

"See what I have in my pocket," Jack said. He showed the princess the gold apple and told her how he got it.

She clapped her hands. "Jack, your kind heart may win the day yet."

 ack and the princess wandered until the sky grew gray. Just when Jack feared they
had failed, they found the unicorn, drinking cool clear water from a pool. Jack
held the gold apple out on his trembling palm. The unicorn raised his head, and came,
timidly, towards them.

When the unicorn took the apple, he became as tame as a cat. At that moment, the
magician appeared. "Now, Jack," he said, "give the unicorn to me."

"That I will not," Jack replied.

The magician raised his staff.

"Quick, Jack," the princess cried. She sprang onto the unicorn's back and gave Jack her hand.

They rode out of the forest, onto a flat grassy plain. "Look back," the princess said, "and tell me what you see."

"The magician is behind us, running faster than a mortal man."

The princess pulled the ribbon from her hair. "Throw this down," she said. Jack did, and it became a great river. "What do you see now?" she asked.

"The magician turned into a salmon," Jack replied, "but we're getting away."

"Good!" said the princess, but she didn't slacken their pace.

After a time, Jack looked back again. "The magician is closer now," he said.

"Throw down my necklace," the princess said. The glittering garnets became a field of red hot stones. But the magician turned into a dragon and skipped over them. "He's getting near now!" Jack cried, feeling the dragon's hot breath behind them.

The princess handed Jack her comb. When he threw it down, a thicket of thorns sprang up, but the magician became a rabbit.

Soon Jack said, "He's out of the thicket. But look! A great eagle is swooping down." They turned and watched as the eagle carried the rabbit away. "That," said the princess, "is the end of him," and she urged the unicorn home.

When they reached the great town, Jack said, "I'll just find my brothers and be on my way."

"That you will not," the princess said, "for where am I to find another man as kind and brave as you, Jack? Stay and help me rule."

So Jack stayed. When his brothers were freed from the quarry, Jack would have kept them near. But after the princess grew to know them, she sent them to govern over the northernmost reaches of her realm. There they lived quite comfortably, their mother with them.

Jack and the princess ruled wisely and were well loved. In time, they married. Their children were kind as their father and clever as their mother and as brave as both. And they all lived the happiest of ever afters.

The End